13.95

10   9   8   7   6   5   4   3   2   1   90B2061

First published in the United States, Great Britain, Canada, Australia and
New Zealand in 1989 by North-South Books, an imprint of Rada Matija AG

Library of Congress Cataloging in Publication Data

Hol, Coby.
   A visit to the farm.
   Translation of: Der Sonnenhof.
   Summary: Julie and Martin see a variety of animals
when they visit the farm to get a basket of eggs and
cheese and a pail of fresh milk.
   [1. Domestic animals--Fiction.   2. Farm life--
Fiction]   I. Title.
PZ7.H688Vi   1989   [E]   88-25366
ISBN 1-55858-000-X

British Library Cataloguing in Publication Data

Hol, Coby, *1943–*
   A visit to the farm.
   I. Title   II. Der Sonnenhof, *English*
   741
   ISBN 1-55858-000-X

A Visit to the Farm

Written and Illustrated by
Coby Hol

North-South Books

New York

Julie and Martin were very excited. Their mother had said they could go to the farm all by themselves to get eggs, cheese and milk.

They had been to the farm many times with their mother. They loved watching the animals and helping to feed them.

First, Martin visited the guinea pig that belonged to the farmer's son. The guinea pig always liked it when Martin picked him up and stroked his soft fur.

Julie went out into the meadow to visit her old
friend Flora, the cow. Julie had known Flora since
she was a calf.

Martin watched the chickens as they picked
and scratched at seeds on the ground.
The rooster stood nearby and made sure that
none of the chickens ran away.

Julie had brought some salt for the goats. They all gathered around and licked the salt from her hand.

"I'm going to see the pigs," yelled Martin. "Mary had babies last week."

Martin gave the little pigs some bread. They pushed their noses through the fence and sniffed it first. "You look so funny with your noses sticking out," said Martin.

Julie went with Martin to visit their favorite animals, the rabbits.

Julie fed the rabbits some dandelions she had picked in the meadow.

Martin carefully took a little white rabbit out of its cage. "I wish I could take you home with me," said Martin. "But I know you would miss all your friends."

Martin walked to the little stream that ran behind the barn. He threw some bread into the water for the goose and the ducks.

Julie heard the farmer taking his horse out of the barn and she ran over to help. The farmer let her lead the horse out into the meadow.

Across the meadow, she saw the farmer's son, kneeling by the pond. He was gently holding a little green frog in his hands. The boy let Julie touch the frog's smooth skin.

"I like frogs," said Julie, "especially when they jump."

The boy opened his hands and the frog leaped through the air, into the cool water of the pond.

"Martin's calling," said Julie. "I think it's time to go home."

Everything was ready. The farmer's wife gave Martin a pail full of fresh milk. Julie took the basket full of eggs and cheese. And they both got a juicy apple to eat on the way home.

"Thank you for letting us play with the animals," said Julie.

The farmer's wife smiled and said, "You can come anytime."